Edited by Aquila Editing

Cover Designer: Cover Girl Design

Hello from Abby!

Thanks for picking up my book! If you want to check out more of my titles and get some free stuff, please visit my author page at www.authorabbyknox.com.

Happy reading!

HAND Tossed

ABBY KNOX

Summary

Diana

First thing to know about me? I don't need an older man with money to solve my problems. And yet, men my own age seem to constantly disappoint, mistreat, and even get me into trouble with the law. My family has helped me before, but I'm determined to stand on my own two feet this time. I'm getting a second job and I'm going to dig myself out of my worries, no matter what it takes. My new boss, however, has other plans. He doesn't understand that my problems are none of his business, and I don't understand his motives. He's going to have to convince me there's more to him than just a guy with impressive moves in the kitchen.

Leo

Life has been good to me so far. My successful pizzeria is the talk of the town and I have everything a man could need or want. What I don't have is a good enough reason to show up single to the family reunion. Again. Finding true love is not all that easy when all I do is work. Turns out, I don't need to try to find it, because when Diana walks into my restaurant looking for a second job, I've found my missing piece. Everything about us makes sense, and I'm determined to show her I'm more than just the guy holding the dough; I'm going to be there for her, through thick and thin.

Chapter One

Diana

"MOM'S GOING to lose her shit," she says.

I touch my newly dyed jet-black hair as I look back at my sister Chloe on the video call.

At 25, I've always been the black sheep of the family. I may as well own it.

"Tell me something I don't know."

Chloe laughs, "I will. How about I'm pregnant, and you're the first to know."

I have to try hard not to roll my eyes. "Again!?" I try to sound happy for my favorite sister, but it comes out a little too exasperated. I mean, this is baby number three for her, and my next older sister, Cara, just had baby number two.

"I can't believe I'm going to be an aunt five times over," I say. "I'm too young for this."

Chloe clucks at me. "Next time, try, 'Congratulations, Chloe,' or 'wow, I'm so excited to welcome the little one into the family.' This is what normal people say when they hear baby news."

Chloe is the only sister who can speak to me like this without making me want to scratch her eyes out. Cara, the goody-two-shoes of the family, always made me appear extra troublesome by comparison. I came into the world screaming, and I've never stopped causing drama. That's what my mother likes to tell me.

I have to say, though, after marrying Dad's best friend four years ago, Cara sure took the focus off of me for a while. I guess I should thank her for that.

The truth is, I'm excited for Chloe. I love her kids. I'm just sad they're all in England, and I'm stuck here in the suburbs, still unsure what to do with my life.

I just can't seem to stop getting into trouble.

"At your age, the shenanigans aren't cute anymore," Mom said the last time we had Sunday night family dinner.

Harsh, but she's right. And she doesn't even know the half of it.

I know if I said the word, Chloe would let me stay with her in England and disappear from my problems for a while. But I can't do that without a work visa. Or with the criminal record I currently have. Fucking Gary.

Everyone thinks I'm such a rebel, but the truth is, I just keep meeting the wrong people. I attract losers. One after another, men screw me over. Cheat, destroy my credit, get me in trouble with the law.

"I'm happy for you guys. Really," I say, grateful for the lag in the FaceTime call that hides the wistfulness in my voice. "As soon as I get my shit together, I'll be expecting some super-posh hand-me-downs for my own offspring," I tell her.

No one knows when that will be. Not even I know

when my shit will get sorted out. If I asked Chloe for money, she would help me immediately. And so would Cara. Neither Phillip nor Michael, their husbands, respectively, would bat an eye at the expense it would take to pull me out of my misery.

Neither would my mom and dad. But those two? If I spilled the whole truth of my situation, I'd have to look at their disappointed faces. My heart can't take it. Even if the charges against me are a huge misunderstanding of the situation. Mom and Dad didn't believe me that my grade-school nemesis started a fight by scuffing up my brand new sneakers, because my nemesis ended up worse off than I did. Dad had to write a check to the little fiend's dad to cover the cost of stitches in the emergency room after I pushed her off the merry-go-round. That incident was the start of it all.

Then a few years back, when my boyfriend cheated on me, I set his car on fire. Mom and Dad took me in and helped me navigate court appearances. I think they both secretly took my side on that one, for once.

Time after time, they have cleaned up my messes, quietly accepting that I was at fault. I was a terror at home with my sisters, so why should I be different in school?

If any of my family members knew the extent to which I've gotten myself buried in court fees, lawyer fees, and back rent after this latest incident, they would jump to help me in a heartbeat.

But I'm tired of being that person. I'm determined to handle all of this on my own.

"Oh, I wish you would hurry up," Chloe says, batting away a Nerf ball. Off-screen, some little monster laughs. Chloe looks off in that direction and shouts, "I told you two no Nerf inside the house!"

She turns back to me and pleads, "I want Katie and Rufus to grow up being best friends with all their cousins."

I sigh and nod, wondering how I would ever meet a nice enough man to help me make mine and my sister's dreams come true. Nice men aren't interested in a girl with a checkered past.

Maybe I should try artificial insemination and cut out the middle man altogether. Yeah right. Try affording that one on a cheap motel housekeeper's wages. A cheap motel that doesn't even let me live there rent-free just because I work there.

Which reminds me, I need to hang up the phone and apply for a second job.

"Good luck!" Chloe waves. I blow kisses at Chloe and the twins, who have appeared on screen to say goodbye to their Aunt Diana.

Moments later, I'm in my beat-up Ford Fiesta and on the road to Leo's Pizzeria to interview for the delivery driver position. I pray to whoever will listen that I can work there just long enough to earn some extra tips to earn first and last month's rent and move out of the fleabag motel.

And then, I pray some more. This time, that I won't end up delivering pizza to a police officer.

Technically, I'm not supposed to be driving a car due to the ongoing case against me. But I know this town's byways and alleyways better than the cops, so I'm pretty sure I can make this work.

What could go wrong, right?

A lot, Diana. A whole hell of a lot could go wrong.

Chapter Two

Leo

I DRAW a line in the sand at illegal activity at my establishment. And my grandfather knows it.

Giving him my final answer to his request, I crank up the opera on my restaurant sound system to drown him out.

Pops should know by now that neither I nor anyone else in the family wants anything to do with the illegal poker games that Pops has gotten himself into. My two brothers' security firm, Parisi International, has been busy enough trying to stay on the good side of the cops who throw them a bone once in a while, and none of us need any funny business.

My grandfather replies by launching a tirade about what I owe him. I go back to tossing my famous pizza dough and drowning my soul in Pavarotti while he rants.

I can't make out exactly what he's saying anymore

because I'm in the zone, and nobody and nothing can harm my zen.

They all try. Pops, my brothers, my sisters, my ma. Everyone. They don't understand why I work my ass off in the food industry. It's tougher than keeping tabs on a bunch of novice gumshoes, that's for sure. But office work doesn't interest me.

Pizza is an art. Kneading the dough, whirling it in the air until it gets to just the proper thinness, and creating world-class food is my art. At the age of 35, I can't imagine doing anything else.

Pizza and occasional trips into the city to see some opera—that's all I need to be happy. Entertaining the dinner crowd with my over-the-top dough throwing isn't a bad gig either. I admit it; it's good for the ego as well as fun. What could be better than feeding people? Just like my brothers, I, too, have an instinct to take care of people.

When he seems to have calmed down, I turn down the music so I can hear. Pops reminds me, "Family is more important than work. This could all go away someday. Look what happened to your cousin's dry-cleaning business."

I shake my head. Pops fails to mention that the laundry business was literally being used to launder his profits from the illegal gambling, and it got raided by the cops.

"It's just a friendly game of poker among old pals!"

I brighten up. "Oh, if that's the case, then you can use your house. I'll even cater it for you."

He wags his finger at me. "You know that's not going to happen."

I laugh and continue whacking the tight ball of dough against the worktop.

"I think we both know why that is, Papa," I say, pushing the dough across the work surface a little too aggressively. My grandmother would suffocate him in his sleep if he brought his bullshit into her house.

"If you won't help, consider yourself disowned…."

He goes through this once a month or so, then he wears himself out and leaves me alone for another month.

Pops shuffles off, and I crank the music back to my preferred volume, just in time for my sister Vicki to call me.

"Are you coming to the family reunion?"

"I have to work," I say, holding the phone between my chin and my shoulder as I continue to work the dough.

"It's your restaurant."

"Yeah. It's pretty much what I live and breathe."

"If you got into the family business, you could have ten private investigators reporting to you, and you could just cash a check and get on with your life. Then you could come with us to the family reunions whenever you wanted."

"Vicki, I gotta go."

"Oh, while I have you on the phone, can I place an order?"

Chuckling to myself, I scribble down her order. Family and friends love to try to get to the head of the line.

I hang up the phone with my sister, and I'm about to turn up the Pavarotti again when I hear something else that makes my fingers pause on the volume button.

A woman's voice. A low, slightly husky voice full of melody and mystery and a hint of trepidation. A voice that could convince me up is down and the sky is purple.

Who is that? I have to know.

I spin around and peek out the kitchen door, scanning the dining area. Toby's interviewing a prospective delivery driver, and running through the usual list of questions.

"Do you have a license and a reliable form of transportation?"

"I do. Yep, I most certainly do."

There are very few people in this world that could actually make me turn down Pavarotti.

I need to hear more. I need to get a look at her.

Easing around the corner, I see her—the most striking woman I've ever laid eyes on is applying for a job as a delivery driver in my restaurant.

Her body language alone announces that she needs this job in a bad way. Her hand fidgets with her long jet-black hair that hangs down the back of a slightly-worn blazer that looks two sizes too large for her frame. Oh, she's definitely going to be working for us. Immediately.

"We'll have to run a background check, of course, then get back to you."

I step forward and hold out my hand. Toby sees me and says to the woman, "Oh, excuse me a minute."

Realizing what I want, he hands me the job application that the woman has just filled out.

I take the paper, and she turns around to look at me. She levels me with a grayish blue gaze, an arresting color against the layered mop of blue-black hair.

Perched on a barstool, I can see a chest tattoo peeking out of the tee-shirt she wears under her blazer. I can't tell for sure but from here the tattoo looks like a skull filled in with rainbow colors.

The two of us lock eyes, and it's all over for me.

I don't care about boss/employee ethics. Suddenly it seems time for me to have a life outside of work.

I don't know if I've ever believed in love at first sight, but it happened that way for my Pops and Grandma. For all his faults, he did one thing right by spotting the love of his life at a casino in Vegas fifty years ago and going for it.

Maybe it is real. Love at first sight happens in opera all

the time. Well, so does dying of consumption, curses, and ghosts.

If it's not love at first sight, it's got to be something. I need to know this woman, and the only way my light-headed brain knows how to make that happen is by giving her the job. That will literally keep her in my contacts.

Ethics be damned.

If all goes well, if my gut is right, maybe I'll even have a date for the family reunion this time.

Maybe for the rest of my life.

Chapter Three

Diana

"COME WITH ME, PLEASE."

The deep, gravelly voice comes from the man in the apron who has peeked out of the kitchen. Oh, I've seen this man before, tossing dough around the kitchen like it's a freakin' frisbee.

Right away, I can see he's a guy who takes no shit. I rub my thumb in the center of my palm, a nervous tic I've developed when I'm not telling the whole truth. Can he tell I wrote some bullshit on my job application?

I may have fudged a little on my interview. Technically I do have a license. It's a suspended license, but I'm hoping to clear that up as soon as possible. If that weasel ex of mine, Gary, ever shows his face.

Hesitantly, I stand and follow the man to his office, which is through the kitchen and down a small dark hallway at the back of the restaurant. When it comes to men, my tattered instincts tell me maybe it's not the best idea to go into a dark hallway alone with a strange man. But to my relief, he leaves the door open and sits far away from me, on the other side of an ugly metal desk. While I sit there in silence and he glances through my papers, I notice his hair. Thick and cropped short, the dark waves are just the kind women love to run their fingers through. His expressive eyebrows say more than the actual words that come from his mouth. He has wide, strong shoulders, almost but not quite like a bodybuilder. He's not exceptionally tall—about my height— but sturdy, a little bit of a soft belly, which I am about eighty percent certain is covered in thick dark fur that would be equally as tempting to run my fingers through. Well, not *my* fingers, per se. But someone's. He wears no wedding ring. Despite the circumstances and forgetting how much of a mess I've made of my life, I still feel a little jolt of happiness that he might not be married.

I can't help myself. "Nice office. No photos of your wife."

"No, not yet."

If Leo unsettled me a minute ago with his orders to follow him alone to his office, the "not yet" with, a slight arc in his eyebrows, screams danger. I'm in freefall without a parachute. Why? How does he transmit a thousand messages with so few words? How does he make me feel all at once that he knows why I'm asking the question, that he forgives me for being nosy, that he's flattered, and that I have something to do with the "not yet" part.

Is this a job interview, or is it some other kind of interview?

"So. Diana."

My spine straightens. Leo's gaze almost feels like a physical presence itself. I can't not make eye contact. It's unnerving, even though he's pleasant enough to look at.

"Diana. It's a beautiful name."

"Thank you."

"Is it a family name?"

"No, my mom chose it for me because I was born the day after the…you know."

Leo's brow furrows like he's trying to figure out a puzzle. "After what?"

"After the princess died. Mom couldn't decide on a name, and then that car accident happened. So, she named me after her."

"That's very sad, and very beautiful."

I've encountered many people who thought my mom's choice of name was morbid. Many more people thought it was inappropriate since the rest of the women in the family have "C" names. Our grandmother thought Mom was marking me for some kind of doom. Looking back on the wreckage of my life so far? Grandma was not wrong.

I am indeed marked for doom. Or chaos, at best.

Leo's kind words make me feel cautiously comfortable as I sit with him. "Thank you, I agree."

We share a silence that's not quite awkward but not quite cozy, either. I think I know what's happening here. He already knows I lied on my application, and he's trying to make me feel better about not giving me the job.

Leo stands without another word, goes to a cardboard box stacked against the wall, and pulls out a ball cap emblazoned with a lion logo and the words "Leo's Pizzeria." "You start now," he says. My jaw drops. "Really?"

"You're surprised." It's not a question.

"I just thought you'd figured out—"

He looks at me curiously, and I say nothing more about what he might have or have not figured out.

"Never mind. Awesome. Thank you so much!"

"No, thank you, Diana."

Moments later, my bewildered and lucky self is back in my car, on my way to my first delivery.

I don't have GPS on this piece of crap car, of course, so I tap the directions into my phone and make my way to the west side of town.

The drive is uneventful and just long enough to allow me to calm my nerves. I deliver the pizza to a nice older woman who gives me a modest tip, and then I make my way to the second stop on the opposite side of town. By this time, I've got the windows cracked, and I'm singing along to my favorite song on the radio, telling myself this is easy. I don't know what I was worried about.

When I arrive at the Main Street address and walk up to the pleasant suburban oak front door, I have no idea what could be waiting for me on the other side. The middle-aged man with a nondescript face looks me up and down.

I force a smile and say, "Medium pepperoni and mushroom?"

He pauses his gaze at my chest, and I wish I hadn't worn this tight tee-shirt with the words stretched across my boobs. But it was the only one clean, and I don't even have money to do laundry right now. My mountaintop mood begins to teeter on the edge of a landslide. It's that pause, combined with a widening of the eyes, the moistening of the lips. I recognize it, and I don't like it. It's the harbinger of unpleasant things about to happen.

"I ordered a pizza, all right," he says, adding, "I didn't know it came with a side of pretty girl." Oh, no.

I stammer and clear my throat. "Just the p-pizza."

He smirks at me and says, "Hold on, I've got your tip in here." The man holds the door wide and invites me to come inside to wait.

"No thanks, I'll just wait right here," I say.

He's already turned away, so he looks at me over his shoulder, "There's no need to wait out there in the heat.

Come on in and have a sweet tea?"

He phrases it like a question, but I can see the strange look on his face, like he will be very pissed off if I don't come in.

The desperate part of me wants to nudge me along.

Just go in and get your tip, Diana. You need every dollar you can get.

Thank god for the still small voice instilled by my parents and older sisters to counteract every one of my terrible instincts. *Sure, you'll have your tip. But no one will ever find your body.*

Thinking quickly, I say, "No, I'm sorry. It's company policy that I do not come inside. I'll wait for my tip right here, thanks."

The man visibly deflates, and then his ears redden with low-boiling anger as he walks away. Meanwhile, I'm still standing here with the pizza in this giant, heavy, insulated sleeve. He makes me wait; it must be five minutes before he returns with a fistful of cash.

"It's really not necessary to tip," I say.

Abruptly, he grabs the pizza before I've even removed it entirely from the sleeve, and shoots me a look as if I've crossed him somehow.

"No, honey. Here you go. You take your tip and run along. May I suggest you buy some modest clothes with it."

He crams the stack of bills into my hand. I want to refuse and throw them back at him, but he's already slammed the door in my face.

My hands shaking, I motor back to Leo's Pizzeria in a fog. This was a terrible idea. This was supposed to be my last-resort job, and I can't even manage to not piss people off doing a straightforward task. Then again, fuck that guy.

None of his business what clothes I wear. Maybe the service industry is not for me if this is how the general public behaves.

When I arrive back at Leo's, the manager, Toby, is waiting for me by the register with a sour look on his face.

"I thought you said you'd done this before," he says.

I open my mouth, ready to defend myself, but I know I have no leg to stand on. He's caught me in a lie. "I'm sorry," I say.

"You look at the orders and take as many as you can," he says, showing me the tickets. "You could have taken these three, then on your way back across town, you would have picked up this fourth order because it's on the way to the third one."

Relieved that he has not, in fact, found me out in a lie, I start to defend myself, but a commanding voice cuts across the dining room.

"Diana? Come with me, please." Again?

Good lord, that man knows how to put me on edge.

As I follow him back to his office for a second time today, I have to ask myself: am I nervous in a dreading kind of way, or is this an excited-to-be-alone-with-him kind of way?

Having just returned from that pretty disgusting inter-action with that pizza customer, I can't trust myself to know the difference at the moment.

Chapter Four

Leo

I DON'T LIKE how spooked Diana looks when she comes back from her first delivery.

She looks only slightly less pale now, back in my office. "Why do you look so freaked out? What happened?"

"This was all a mistake." She proceeds to tell me about a truly horrifying interaction on her second delivery. By the time she's finished her story, my blood boils and my rage pours off me.

"You won't ever have to worry about delivering pizza again to that guy's house."

She protests, "I don't want to piss off the rest of the staff. I can handle him."

I hold up my hand and say, "I'm cutting him off. He's not getting any more food from me. He can keep his money."

Her jaw drops. "I'm costing you money on my first day. This can't be good for business."

"I do what I have to do to protect my staff," I say.

Diana's face is full of regret, and I hate that I've played any role in making her feel that way. "This always happens," she says. "I'm always the centerpiece to whatever drama is going on, and I hate that. I don't want to cause trouble. I just want to pay my bills and be a good person."

I don't know where her feelings of negativity come from, but I intend to find out as soon as possible. I want to know every single thing about this woman.

I stand up and cross over to her, workplace protocols be damned. I sit down next to her and say, "Hold up. You were just doing your job. A customer caused a problem, and I'm fixing it."

She shakes her head and stares at her shoes. "You're more than fixing it. This is above and beyond."

My feelings are all over the place. Anger at that idiot customer. Annoyance at Toby. Curiosity at why she's beating herself up. But I'm determined to make her feel better about what's happening. "I'm responsible for you, Diana."

Her eyes widen, and she finally meets my eyes. I see a tear forming in the corner, and it feels like a punch in the gut. "Be-because I'm your employee? I'm just a delivery driver, and it's my first day. You don't even know me."

"That, and because I can tell something else is going on with you. And I want you to know, I'm gonna take care of everything. Whatever drama you think you're the cause of? You don't have to worry about that anymore."

Diana blurts out a sudden, unexpected laugh, then looks at me skeptically. "You're going to take care of everything? First of all, you have no idea what you're talking about. And second, I appreciate you being a decent employer, but I don't need a man to take care of me and my personal problems."

Against all propriety, I lean in closer, careful not to touch her. But oh man, do I want to touch. I'd love to wrap her up in my arms and inhale her sweet and spicy scent of ginger and dark chocolate. But I can't do that; I shouldn't even be thinking it unless I want to get slapped with a lawsuit. And yet, I can't keep my eyes off those pouty lips, imagining myself catching that full bottom lip in a distracting kiss. At the moment I'd settle for wiping away her tears if that were allowed. I hand her a box of tissues. She takes one out and thanks me. "When I say not to worry about anything, I mean anything. Not ever again.

Now, I'll take the hat back, please."

Diana's gray-blue eyes blink in shock at my outstretched hand. "Oh no. I'm being fired. That's what this is about." She's dabbing tears away while her lovely eyes well up some more.

"Sweetheart. I'm going to teach you how to make pizza."

She looks at me like I've lost my mind. I brace myself for the punch, or the scolding, for calling her "sweetheart." I would deserve it.

"But your sign said you were hiring drivers and wait staff," she points out.

Before I can stop myself, I blurt it all out. "I have to keep my eye on you, Diana. No customers are speaking to you ever again. That's how angry I am at that guy. That's what this is about, okay?"

For a moment, she looks at me like I'm suffering from delusions, then shakes her head in disbelief. "I'm not fired?"

I laugh. "No. You've been promoted."

Chapter Five

Diana

I WATCH in amazement as Leo hands over the rest of the deliveries to the other drivers, as well as an ashen-looking Toby.

And then he insists that I go home and rest up for tomorrow. "Big day. You're going to learn all about how to make pizza, starting with the dough."

He holds open the door, and to my surprise, follows me to my car. He really meant what he said about protecting me. I imagine tomorrow this will wear off after he sees what a disaster I am in the kitchen. My sisters Cara and Cherise know their way around an oven. Me? I'm like I am with everything else—a mess.

Still, tomorrow should be fun while it lasts. I've seen the way this man with his veiny forearms handles dough. My family has visited this restaurant several times over the years, and this man makes theater out of tossing dough in the air. It's like watching a magician.

"You don't need to escort me to my car," I say.

"Yes. I do."

"It's 8 p.m., and it's not dark out."

"So?"

"So I think I'm taking up too much of your time, Leo."

"Wrong," he says, leveling me with a look that sends shivers down my spine as he leans against my car. As I unlock it, I marvel at how much space he takes up. He's not huge or tall, but the way he stands, leans with his whole arm outstretched over the window frame, he looks imposing nonetheless. He's sturdy and thick in all the right places. His scent of woodsmoke and fresh bread makes me feel both hungry and intoxicated.

Before I close the door and drive away, he leans in a little too close to me and says, "You're not taking up nearly *enough* of my time, Diana."

In my rearview mirror, I watch his reflection shrink as I leave Leo's Pizzeria and head out down the street toward home. What is his deal?

It hits me like a bolt of lightning as I sit at the stoplight.

"Oh, Diana. He likes you. You incredible dummy!"

It took me a minute to notice this because I'm too used to creeps being so blatant about hitting on me that I don't discern when a genuinely decent guy shows an interest.

But is he a decent guy? His energy is so dominant and mysterious. *And he's your boss?* Isn't my boss supposed to avoid favoritism?

Hell, it's nice to be the favorite for once. *God, Diana. Middle child, much?*

Should I be entertaining this thought, though? Based on my experience, better to err on the side of extreme caution. But I'm alone at the moment, so I set aside caution and enjoy this feeling.

This man, this bona fide artist, finds me attractive and

would knock someone's lights out for calling me a slut. That's enough to make me enjoy the rest of my evening.

But my enjoyment is soon destroyed, once again, by an unwelcome presence: red and blue lights reflecting against my windshield.

"Oh, fuck."

I pull over and try to breathe. In and out. *It's going to be okay, Diana. You just gotta own up to your mess and explain how you're going to fix it.*

Maybe the cops have a payment plan this time instead of a massive fine? Perhaps the jail is full. Ha.

One can always hope.

Chapter Six

Leo

I GO against everything I stand for when I hop into my car to follow her home.

For the record, I don't do this. I don't follow women home without them knowing about it.

Diana has brought out a beast inside of me that I don't recognize. When she told me what that guy said to her, I wanted to go to his house and punch him in the face. I mean, I want to hit every asshole in the face, but right now, I literally feel ready to fight that douchebag. I could burn his house down and blow up his car, and holy shit…I'm no better than the riff-raff my Pops hangs out with at this point.

I forget about all the things that are wrong with me following her home, and I just go with my instincts. Being close to her, I feel settled. Calm. Centered.

It feels wrong when she's away from me.

What is this? Is it love? Do I actually love this woman

who I can see bopping along to the radio three cars ahead of me with the window open, her blue-black hair flailing around?

When we cross the intersection, a city police car has sidled up right behind Diana's Fiesta and bleats its warning siren.

"Oh shit."

My hackles go up, and I park down the block to watch this play out. What in the world could they be pulling her over for?

I watch as she rolls down her window and gives the officer a hesitant smile. I know that look. She thinks she's guilty of something. She's talking with her hands, and the officer is looking at her driver's license. He gestures at her with it, waving it around in the air, and then heads back to his patrol car, I assume to call it in.

This looks at first like a routine traffic stop, but it's now turned into something else. Diana covers her face with her hands and leans forward against the steering wheel.

She's in trouble.

My brain has left the station; all that's left to manage the tracks is every nerve in my body. I have to close the physical distance between Diana and myself: that's all I know. I have to help her and be close to her. Instinct, passion, feelings have taken over. I'm utterly unregulated.

Leaving my Jeep at the side of the road, I approach the patrol car. This goes against all sound judgment, but there's nothing left upon seeing Diana look troubled.

"That's my employee," I say to the officer. "Is there something I can help with here?"

The officer looks over at me sideways. "Yeah, pal, you could not interfere with police business," the officer says. I read his badge.

"Sgt. Bernard, I'd like to help in any way I can. My employee seems to be down on her luck."

He glances up at me. "You might want to rethink hiring her. She's wanted for missing a court date and has a suspended license from a drunk driving charge."

I said I wanted to get to know Diana; I just didn't think I'd be learning about her through a law enforcement source. Still, there has to be more to this story.

"Are you sure you've got the right girl?"

"Girl," he snickers. "This young lady has been a thorn in the side of this precinct since she was a juvenile. Although the juvie stuff is officially sealed, blah, blah, blah." He uses air quotes around the word "sealed." I do not like that one bit; it implies he and his buddies jaw about everyone's juvenile records.

Suddenly, the police officer's face changes as he studies me. "Wait a minute. You're the pizza guy!"

I nod my head. "Leo," I say, holding out my hand. "I know you; I see you back there in the kitchen, doing your thing...."

What follows is a conversation I have around town every time I'm not in my house or in my work kitchen. Everybody recognizes me as the guy tossing around the pizza dough, and everyone wants to have a conversation about it. And this is why I rarely leave the house.

It's not that I'm a jerk. If I didn't like people, I wouldn't be in the food business. I'm just quickly drained by a lot of people's energy.

Diana is different. I don't feel drained around her. I feel energized. That's why I need to protect her at all costs.

I'm not proud of what happens next. But it's my only option to keep her out of jail.

Namedropping Frank Parisi, my ex-cop brother-turned-security guru has bought Diana some time.

The offer of free pizza for a year doesn't hurt, either.

When the officer drives away, Diana sees me. Her eyes go wide, her mouth drops open, and she hightails it back to my car. I can't tell from the look on her face if she's hopping mad or grateful.

She has every right to be whatever emotion she picks.

Chapter Seven

Diana

"WHAT DID YOU DO?"

Leo lifts one shoulder and looks up at me innocently. "I was just following you home to make sure you were okay."

I squint down at him, revving myself up to really let him have it for sticking his nose where it doesn't belong. For intervening as if I'm some sort of damsel in distress.

To my surprise, he gets out of the car while I'm in the middle of my speech and says, "Passenger side.

Now."

He grips me under my arm and escorts me swiftly to the curb side. "What are you doing!?" I shout.

"It's not safe to have a conversation by the side of the road, especially not on that side. Get in." He holds the door open for me.

"I'm not getting in your car," I say, squaring my shoulders.

"Yes, you are. And then I'm driving you home. And

then I'm taking that rattle trap you call a car to my brother's scrapyard."

"What am I supposed to drive?"

He growls, "I'll pick you up for work tomorrow; now would you get into the car so we can talk?"

"If you expect some kind of repayment for bribing the cops back there, you are sorely mistaken," I say, my voice cracking.

This makes him step back, his face a little hurt.

Instantly, I regret what I said.

What he says next, though, is so perfect it breaks my heart and puts it back together. "Diana, I see you. I understand why you would think that about me or any other guy. And I'm not going to stand here and pretend I'm any different from any other jerk who has mistreated you in the past. So I'm not going to force you into the car. But the truth is, your car is not safe to drive. And you're not allowed to drive, anyway. But I promise you are safe with me. Here," he says, handing his phone out to me. "Call my sister. Her contact is right there. Call her and ask her if I'm safe."

I look at his phone, then up at his face. His words are pleading, but his tone, and his face, are not. He's serious. He does see me. And he doesn't care what I've done or what the police believe I've done.

My hands wave in surrender. "All right. I'll get in the car. We probably do have some things to talk about."

After I get inside and he slides back into the driver seat next to me, I watch as he texts someone then throws the Jeep into gear. He cranks the wheel and heads toward the back of a nearby mini-mall. "Where are you taking me?" I ask.

"Dunkin'. What do you want?" he asks as he eases into the drive-through lane.

I tell him a raspberry jelly, and he orders a sour cream for himself, plus two coffees.

"Coffee, huh? This really is going to be a conversation," I comment.

He winks at me and then parks behind the Dunkin', and we eat our donuts together.

"What's going to happen with my car?"

Leo gestures with his phone. "My brother's gonna have your car towed to his scrapyard. I wasn't kidding about that."

I shake my head. "I don't suppose you're going to listen when I tell you I can't afford to have my car towed."

He shakes his head. "Nope." The grin that follows slams into me with such unexpected sweetness. Why should I be surprised to see him smile? Everything he's done for me today has been massively sweet and above and beyond what an employer should do for his brand new employee.

"What is it you want to do with your life, Diana?"

I shrug and sip my coffee. "Right now, I just want to get my shit together and stay out of trouble. And then I want to find an apartment that allows pets, so I can get a dog."

Leo smiles and listens while I talk about all my immediate needs. Paying my electric bill. Paying off court fines.

Tracking down my ex so he can clear my name.

At his curious expression, I then launch into the whole story. "My ex framed me for drunk driving, but nobody believes me. One night we were at a party. I was bored and not feeling well from the disgusting punch somebody made. Too strong. He was pissed and told me I had to wait. I sort of fell asleep, and the next thing I knew, I was sitting in the driver's seat of Gary's car, being awakened by a policewoman, after the car had crashed into a metal barricade on a country road. Gary was nowhere to be found, and I haven't been able to track him down since then."

I look over, and Leo's eyes could burst into flames. His jaw tics, visible even from under that lovely dark beard. He sets down his coffee and rubs his palm over his face.

"Fucking asshole. Could have gotten you killed." A lump forms in my throat at the memory. "I know. Thank you for saying that."

"Did your parents help you hire a lawyer?"

"I didn't tell them."

"Sweetheart, you gotta tell 'em."

I shake my head. "Can we just not talk about this? I'm already going to have trouble sleeping tonight because my crazy boss just promoted me to line cook or whatever."

Leo's hand is still rubbing his beard as if he's trying to get control of his emotions.

"I'm glad you told me that story. But what I really wanted to know, Diana, what you want to do with your life.

Like, down the line."

I lift one shoulder. "Fuck if I know."

Leo pivots in the seat to lean in closer to me. I can feel his zest for life pouring off of him. I wish I had that. "What have you always wanted to do? What's your passion?" He says the word passion with his whole body, his brows furrowed in challenge and his hand gesturing while gripping the sour cream donut.

I feel heat flood all through me, and I can't tell if it's because it's the first time in a long time that someone has asked me something so deep, or because his attention doesn't creep me out.

The way my heart races when he looks at me with those intense eyes, I don't want to be careful. I can tell he doesn't want to be careful either.

"I've always wanted to go to art school," I say. I can't

believe I said that out loud to someone on the first day of knowing them. How did he make me do that? "But I'm 25, and I think I'm past that now."

"Hold up," Leo says. "If you want to go to art school, you're going to fucking art school. What do you want to do? Paint? Draw?"

I smile shyly. "Sculpt," I say. "But I can't afford art school."

"No, but I can."

I back away from him because suddenly, everything is clear. He's not just interested in me for who I am. It makes sense: showering me with opportunities and making problems disappear. And now, trying to fund my education.

My throat dries up. "Listen, I can't accept your help if this is a sugar daddy type of offer. You will be disappointed at my sexual prowess, I'm just saying."

Leo's brow angles up in confusion. "What? I don't know what you mean by 'sugar daddy.'"

I scoff. "Yes, you do. Everyone knows what that means. An old man offers to pay a young woman's way through school in exchange for her company." Around the word "company," I use air quotes.

This explanation seems to shock him. "Diana." That's all he says, but it says a thousand different things. All of which soothe my unease. He's telling me that's not what this is. That I should know better, and that he would never expect anything in return for his kindness. That he wants me to see him as an equal even though he's my boss.

"I understand why you think that. But no, that's not it."

"You keep saying you understand my reasons for acting or behaving a certain way, and I'm going to fall in love with you, Leo," I joke and then take the last bite of my jelly donut.

He blows out a breath. "Let's hope so."

My gasping causes the last chunk of donut to get caught in my throat. I can't breathe. My hands go to my neck. When Leo sees this, he springs into action, of course. What follows might be the most humiliating moment of my life.

Even more embarrassing than being strip-searched at the precinct.

Leo's thick body is all around me, and his arms surround my torso, his closed fists clasped together in the middle of my sternum. Oh god. I'm either going to barf or crack a rib, and either way, I hope the earth swallows me up when it's over. One quick thrust, and the chunk flies out of my mouth onto the floorboards of the Jeep. Tears stream from my eyes.

"Oh my god, why am I crying?" I mutter between coughs.

"It's your gag reflex; it's normal. Here, drink some water."

Leo sets about cleaning me up and wiping the tears from my cheeks.

"That's one way to ruin a possibly romantic moment, Diana," he says with a smirk.

I can't help but laugh. "You shouldn't have made me laugh in the middle of eating a donut."

He stares me down, and I know from the look in his eye he wasn't joking.

"Well, any romantic things you might have been feeling are surely out the window now, now that I've barfed all over your car."

He's still dabbing my cheek with his thumb, even though I've no tears anymore. "Just a little bit of donut. No big whoop. Worse things have occurred in this Jeep. A lot messier things."

I don't know why my mind goes there, but I do not

want to think about him having sex with other women, especially not here in this Jeep, where I'm sitting.

"Whoa," I say. "I think it's time for me to go home."

I stay silent and think things over as we make our way to the shitty motel. When we arrive, I say, "Wait a minute. How did you know where I live?"

"It's on your job application, and I already Google-Mapped it." "Creepy," I tease.

He lifts one shoulder in acknowledgment. "Runs in the family. By the way, I don't like this neighborhood." "It's all I can afford," I say.

"Let's talk more later tonight."

I shake my head. "Whatever, Leo. I hope you're not expecting a kiss goodnight after I horked up a donut."

"No, but I am expecting a phone call when it's time for bed."

"Why?"

"So I can confirm with you that my family's security guys drive by the house while they're on the job tonight."

"Are you kidding me?"

"Meh. They're over here often enough catching bail skips. It won't be like they're going out of their way." "None of this makes me feel any better," I say.

"Good night, Diana."

The trembling is from the choking scare, I tell myself. Not because the more protective Leo gets, the more I want him.

I go inside and lock the door behind me.

I kick off my shoes, gather my pajamas, and get ready for a night in front of the television. Cara was nice enough to give me her streaming service password to at least enjoy some entertainment. While I'm pulling down my pajama top, I see a shadow across the window, nearly giving me a heart attack. "Holy shit!"

And that's when I peek through the blinds and see who it is. Leo is checking to make sure all my doors and windows are locked. I don't say anything. I know there's nothing I can do to make him calm down.

I have to admit to myself it feels good to have someone be so protective of me. As I watch Leo drive away, I try to identify this feeling that I'm having.

It's goodness. Not since I lived with my family have, I felt this. Like I'm almost home.

Chapter Eight

Leo

I CRACK open my second beer of the night and sip from the brew as I wait for Diana to call.

My brother Christopher calls while I pace around the pool in the backyard. He lets me know he's got Diana's car at the scrapyard.

"Thanks, brother. Just hold tight until we get the title and everything switched over."

Christopher has a few questions for me. Of course, he does; he's related to me.

"What's the deal? I don't mind holding on to some chick's car; I'm sure you got your reasons. I just wanna make sure everything is on the up and up." I snort.

"Dude, it's not of my business, but I gotta ask just like I would if it was anybody else telling me to keep a car off the street."

This makes sense. "I get it, Christopher. The woman it belongs to is in some trouble, and I'm helping her out. If people see her car on the street, she might never drive again."

"Cop troubles. I hear ya," Christopher says. "So, are you going to tell me about the girl?"

"There's nothing to tell."

Christopher laughs. "Sure, sure. You involve your brother in helping you take care of problems with just any woman who walks into your pizza establishment off the street. I get it."

"It's very new, and I don't want to jinx it by saying too much."

Christopher pauses, and I wait for the wisecrack. But he doesn't make one. Instead, he says, "I hope we all get to meet her at the family reunion."

I hold my breath, still expecting the punchline that never comes.

"I'm planning on it," I tell him.

We hang up, and it's clear that my brother heard something in my voice that wasn't there before.

I flip through my choices on TV, but nothing grabs my attention. Waiting for her to call me tonight is excruciating.

I pace around my house, repeatedly checking my phone. After a couple of hours, I start to think she's not going to call.

Stepping outside to stare at the small backyard pool that I never use, I think I must have screwed up somehow.

You blew it, man. You said too much, and you freaked her out.

Just as I'm about to give up and head inside, away from the mosquitoes, her number appears.

She doesn't even say hello; she just jumps right in. "Why did you hire me on the spot?"

"And good evening to you, Diana," I reply.

"Are you going to answer the question?"

I smile as I get myself ready for bed. I hate placing her

on speaker while I do my nighttime routine, which makes me notice how much I enjoy her voice up close to me.

"I knew you were a good fit," I say.

"Bullshit. You thought my car was a death trap, and you could see on my job application I had no experience in the food industry. Now tell me the real reason."

I spit out my toothpaste in the sink and clean myself up, taking a sip of water. I take her off speaker and look at myself in the mirror. That is the face of a man who is about to give up the truth.

"Because I was attracted to you as soon as I met you."

"Do you see how sexist that is?"

"I don't care. And it's not just because you're a woman and it's not just your looks. You're just an objectively attractive, intriguing human and I didn't want you to leave."

Diana's voice sounds slightly indignant. "Listen. I can't have you fighting my battles. I can't have you solving my problems with money. It's weird and creepy, and I already watched two of my sisters let older men change their life with money, and I don't want that for myself."

As I strip off my clothes and get ready to shower, I have to ask the obvious question. "Tell me, would your sisters have fallen in love and married these men if they had no money?"

"Yes."

"So your sisters are not as shallow as you think."

"Dude, why are you busting my chops so hard?" she says with a laugh.

"I don't know. Every time I try to have a romantic moment with you, one of us fucks it up," I say.

"Throwing up will do that."

"Hey," I say, turning on the spray. "At least now I've

already seen you at your worst, which was still pretty fuckin' sexy, to be honest."

"Why do you have to be like that?"

"Like what?"

"Pushy, forward, demanding but yet also so sweet that I'm waiting for the ax to fall."

I hate that she feels that way, but there's nothing I can do to change that but be who I am. "Baby, no axes are falling anywhere near you as long as I'm in your life."

She sighs heavily, and I can't tell if it's a swooning sigh or an "I'm going to regret this" sigh. "Why did I have a feeling you were going to say that?"

I reply, waiting for the water to heat up, "Because I'm predictable. That's my goal. I'm not going to pull any shady shit on you. I'm your brick wall, baby."

She says, "I believe you, but I feel bad getting you involved in my situation."

"I'm here by choice. And I believe you. What's Gary's last name?"

She tells me, and that's all I need.

"Thanks, doll."

"Why did you need to know that?"

"Have a good night. See you in the morning."

I don't know if she meant to keep me on the phone until I can hear her sleeping, but I'm glad she does. It hurts to hang up after listening to her even breathing for about thirty minutes, but then I have another phone call to make.

Chapter Nine

Diana

WHEN I ARRIVE at work the following day, Leo is waiting for me in the kitchen with a mischievous look on his face.

"For the record, since I'm trying complete honesty now, I know nothing about making pizza," I tell him.

"For the record, your skill level doesn't matter; as you probably know by now, this promotion is a ploy to keep an eye on you."

He hands out a white double-breasted jacket and I take it, saying, "Cherise is going to kill me for having the audacity to wear one of these."

He raises one eyebrow while helping me button the buttons, and I explain that sister number four went to culinary school.

"Well, what she doesn't know won't hurt her," Leo says. As he says this, his hand accidentally brushes against my breast. My cheeks explode with red, and I look down at our hands grappling with the large buttons, and I decide to not acknowledge what has just happened.

He definitely accidentally grazed my boob last night while saving me from choking to death, so maybe just get over it, Diana. Tell that to my hardening nipples, which only grow harder as I look down at our hands fussing with these buttons.

"I-I got it," I say.

"Stop," he chuckles, and the throbbing between my thighs says, *yes, sir. Have at it.*

Oh god, look at how capable his fingers are up close as he manhandles my silly jacket. He could toss me around the bed with those hands as artfully as he tosses pizza dough. Veiny, angular, and softened with black fuzz on the back. Leo's hands might go slow buttoning me up, but I bet they could rip all these layers of clothing off me in seconds.

I shouldn't be thinking these things while at work. I have to stop looking at those sexy hands, so I look at Leo's face. He's so close there's nowhere else to look. Leo's thick brows knit together in concentration, and I have to stop myself from gasping when I notice just how clear and lovely his skin is. His expressive forehead sparks an urge in me to lean forward an inch and kiss him there. And then, the point of his tongue peeks out from between his lips in concentration.

"God, how many buttons are on this thing?"

Leo laughs. "There, done." He smooths the fabric down my arms and meets my gaze. This time I gasp almost audibly at those intense eyes of his. His hands still rubbing down my arms, it feels like he's daring me to look away.

"Time to make the pizza?" I say, a little bit raspy and a lot too sexy.

Leo's teeth bite down on his bottom lip as he reaches up toward my face and moves a strand away from my eyes.

"You got one of those things? To pull your hair back?"

Snapping back to reality, I nod. "Yeah. Yeah, I do." I step away and catch my breath while I put my hair up in a top knot.

No surprise, Leo is a patient, gentle teacher when teaching the art of pizza dough.

He talks me through the process of combining ingredients while he shoves wood into the brick oven on the far side of the kitchen.

"Are you sure you don't want to monitor this and make sure I don't murder your yeast?"

He laughs. "I got plenty more where that comes from. Not to brag, but I make my own yeast, so I always have some started, in different stages."

I fold the ingredients together in a bowl and say, "A scientist and an artist. Impressive."

He walks back over to the prep area, smelling like a wood fire, and washes his hands.

"Nah," he says. "I'm just picky and overbearing."

"You don't say," I tease, looking at him sideways while I stir.

Leo crowds me. I can feel his body heat from inches away. Strangely, I think he would be easier to resist if he were taller. I could avoid him staring at me like that.

He compliments my technique, then spreads flour all over the prep space. "Tip it out, and we'll get started with the fun part."

Leo speaks those words so close to me, my whole body reacts. It's as if his words can physically prod all the places I had shut down after Gary screwed me over. Everything is waking up, and my well of jokes about Leo's scrutiny has run out. My throat dries up, blood rushes to all the places below my navel, my skin wants to be touched.

Dough, Diana. We're just making dough here.

"Now watch me," he instructs.

Gladly.

I'm supposed to be learning how to knead the dough, but mostly all I do is watch his arms ripple while he does everything by hand.

Was I fantasizing about his strong fingers ripping my clothes off a minute ago? Well, now his arms are putting much dirtier thoughts into my head. I stare, wide-eyed and wordless, as Leo bangs the stiff dough ball against the edge of the countertop.

Bangs. There's no other word for it. He's banging dough, and the sound echoes off the tile walls. I feel like I shouldn't be watching this part; it's almost violent.

The flexing of his arms in that sleeveless shirt, combined with that apron, is a whole entire look. Is that even allowed? Surely looking like a beefier Matt Dillon in the Outsiders must be a health code violation. It's definitely a violation of my virginity because, in my mind, those arms are already lifting me up on this workspace, spreading me wide, keeping me still so he can do a hundred different filthy things.

"Would you like me to guide your hands?"

"Excuse me?" It's then I realize he's stopped banging the dough, and he's talking to me.

He smiles and beckons me with one flour-covered finger. "C'mere."

"Where do I…?"

"Stand here," he says, pointing to a spot right in front of him.

"You mean *Ghost* style?" He smirks. "I guess."

I bite my lip as I remember the scene from the movie I just brought up. A jolt of electricity runs down my back.

Leo reaches around with me positioned in front and

blankets my hands with his, guiding me through the movements.

My body stiffens with the back-and-forth motion of the kneading, but his warmth, his masculine scent, the sound of the romantic opera music on the sound system, and his narration in my ear help me relax and ease into the rhythm with him. Together, we make the dough submit to our will.

He keeps going, telling me all the steps involved. "I'm never going to remember any of this," I tell him.

"I'm right here, Diana. I'll always be right here."

I did not give my throat permission to form a little lump just now. "Why do you have to be so sweet?"

"Would you rather I behave like an asshole? Is that what you're used to?"

Back and forth, his thick hands push the meat of my palms into the dough, and then we pull back and do it again. The little ball is going soft and stretchy. His movements with my hands feel like a meditation.

"Yeah, I'm used to assholes. You being so sweet and so…close to me…is making it hard to see the bad stuff, if you even have any bad stuff."

I try not to reveal how he's causing my breath to go shallow or my pulse to quicken, but I'm not sure he's buying it.

"Does it feel good to be treated the way you deserve, Diana?"

"It does feel good," I whisper, my throat fully closed up with emotion.

I look over my shoulder to meet his eyes, which are on me instead of the dough.

"Shouldn't you be watching what we're doing?"

"I can do this in my sleep," he says. "Some days, I

wake up kneading the pillow on the empty side of the bed."

Our hands pause in the soft, elastic dough, and I notice his fingers are threaded through mine. My body temperature seems to be on the rise, or the brick oven has gotten far too hot.

"That should be sad, but you made that image sound pretty hot," I admit. The truth is, all I can think about now is what if I was on the other side of that bed. What if I woke up to the sensation of those strong hands kneading, prodding, working over my body in the middle of the night? Here in stark reality, under the fluorescent lights of his kitchen, we can't get that far.

His breath wafts against my cheek. "I think we're ready for the next step."

My pussy contracts with this suggestion, totally confused by what he meant.

"Are you sure?" My eyes drop to his lips. Leo notices, and I feel his body impossibly grow three inches taller. His arms feel bigger, his torso wider, his breadth more imposing. Leo surrounds me with all of him, and standing there just like that, our lips connect in a searching kiss.

Everything is warm and spicy, and the world feels like it could be full of good things. No, I know it is. I've always known a connection could be this good, but here with Leo, with his lips so tenderly exploring mine, I know it to be the most profound connection of my life. I'm getting ready to jump in with both feet, and I'm grateful that it doesn't feel like I'm jumping in headfirst.

Leo swipes lips across mine and cups my face. The move squeezes out the last of my resistance, and I melt against his chest.

My hands are still buried in the dough, which feels extra

heavy as I let it hold me in place. Leo snakes an arm around my waist, under my apron. He gently tugs me flat against his hard chest, and I melt further against this solid wall of man. He's taken over all of my senses, and I never want it to end.

The sweetness of the moment takes a turn toward passion when I feel something rigid against my lower back. Leo's hand at the front of my waist slips just under the hem of my tee-shirt. Involuntarily I push back against his hard length, and the man exhales a soft groan into my mouth. Letting go of my cheek, he frees my hands from the dough, then spins me to face him. I expect him to go right back in for a deeper kiss, but he pauses to look at me.

Just…look at me.

I should bolt right now. I can't handle such intense eye contact even on my best day. This is so much. His eyes travel over my hair, cheekbones, mouth, ears, jawline, as if he's mapping me out. He's deciding which route to take to my heart, but what he doesn't know is, he's already there.

He closes in for another kiss just as the phone rings. Cursing, he then proceeds to kiss me anyway, this time with a bit more passion behind it. My thighs, knees, even my feet feel a rush of electricity with Leo's lips on mine.

Unable to ignore the phone any longer, he pulls away from the kiss. I look at the clock as he answers.

Oh right. This is a place of business.

And that's when I realize this man, intentionally or not, is going to keep me as horny as a cat in heat all goddamn afternoon and evening until closing time.

If Leo weren't so sweet, I'd be mad as hell.

Chapter Ten

Leo

THE REST of the afternoon until the dinner rush arrives is torture. On purpose.

Images run through my head in cycles: Diana making a ruckus with me in my bed. Diana bent over this work surface. Diana riding me cowgirl style in my meat freezer. I don't care where or what position, as long as it's me and her.

But she's a scared little bunny; I have to make her come to me.

That kiss, those soft, sweet lips against mine, those curves melding into all my angles, sent the signal. She's ready to want me.

Which means I get to make her beg.

At first, I'm a good boy. I do nothing but catch her eye from time to time as we move around each other in the kitchen. A wink here. A smile there. I let her turn around to see me biting my lip while staring at her cute little butt.

While I take orders on the phone, I make sure she sees me stroking my beard while I let my eyes drift down below her middle.

Her cheeks blaze when she realizes what I'm implying, and she spills a whole jar of my homemade pizza sauce on a prepared crust.

"Oh shit!"

I saunter over and touch her lower back. She jumps at my touch. "It's fine." I help her clean it up and tell her we can save that pizza just for us.

"After closing," I say, close to her ear.

The time is approaching the dinner rush, which means the rest of the night should fly under the most uncomplicated circumstances. Tonight, it's going to be delicious torment instead.

I just need one more hot kiss before the hungry hordes show up. I've got her crowded against the counter, my hands locked on either side of her. Diana releases a tiny whimper and leans in for a kiss. How can I resist? Our lips locked together is complete perfection, and I want to drown myself in her. But I have to keep control of the situation. As much as I don't want to, I pull back.

"Why'd you stop, Leo? You're making me crazy."

"Because we can't do this here," I reply, brushing my fingers along her cheekbones.

She sighs. "Then why do you keep looking at me like that? Brushing past me. Standing so close. It's…it's…."

I kiss the tip of her nose while she adorably grunts in frustration. "Be a good girl, and the boss will reward you later."

Not going to lie; her small, quiet moan makes me feel ten feet tall. I let go of her face and watch as her eyes drift down my body. I know she sees what's going on under this apron, inside my jeans. I know she feels it every time I stand behind her in the kitchen to coach her with a new batch of dough.

"I thought you were a sweetheart," she whispers against my neck. I close my eyes and feel her breath tickle my skin. "What are we doing? We should be keeping our distance. This is unprofessional."

I grit out, "This is foreplay, baby. Hasn't anyone done this to you before?"

She smirks. "No, but there's a good reason—"

Just then, the hostess startles us both out of our little game by throwing open the kitchen shutters.

That's right. It's Friday night.

"Showtime," I say.

She whines as I back away from her, but not enough to hide from everyone what we've been doing back here.

"Diana!"

My girl's eyes widen in horror, but she doesn't turn around. "What is it, baby?"

Diana closes her eyes in frustration.

"My mother."

Chapter Eleven

Diana

MY PARENTS and my two younger sisters have decided to have dinner at Leo's Pizzeria tonight, and if you could produce a tutorial about how to throw cold water on a person's sex drive, this would be it.

"Mother, what are you doing here?"

The woman who birthed me and who has spent every day since then trying to embarrass me is standing right in front of the window. The window that all the customers came here for, to watch Leo do his magical dough-tossing routine while they eat their pizza. Other customers are muttering about her being in the way.

"I called to order a pizza to be delivered by my daughter, but they said you'd been promoted to the kitchen. So we came to see for ourselves!"

I sigh, though I shouldn't be surprised. I'm sure she found out through Chloe. I can tell she's proud of me, so I try not to give her too much of a hard time.

"Well, thank you, but Leo's gotta do his thing, and you're kind of in the way, Mom. I'm sorry."

She looks past me and waves to Leo. I squeeze my eyes shut. This can't be happening. Behind me, Leo says, "You must be Diana's mom. So nice to meet you, Mrs. Williams."

When I open my eyes, my mother is giving me a knowing look. I look past her, and my sisters watch in amusement, and Dad with interest to see what's going to happen next.

Mom whispers loudly, "Actually, it looks like you might be the one getting in the way. With your mouth."

"Mom."

She waves again. "Okay, okay. I'll be good. You be good too!" The wink she gives me is a little over the top.

Can I crawl into the meat freezer and die now?

Sensing my embarrassment, Leo rests his hand on my hip, leans in, and says in my ear, "Everyone knows now. How does that feel?"

Turning my head over my shoulder, I reply, "Knows what?"

"That I'm your guy."

All logic would tell me to run. That you can't be in a relationship with someone after one day. But how much more does he have to prove himself? It's not as if I enjoy waiting for my life to happen.

Things are starting to fall into place. And no, I'm not a damsel in distress. I was drowning, and he threw me a rope because he's a human being with the means to help.

I smile at him. He looks so happy and carefree. He doesn't care what anyone thinks. He didn't even blink at meeting my mother unexpectedly. I've never met anyone like him, and I don't think I ever will again.

Finally, I grab the rope and hold on. "Good. It feels good."

His fingertips brushing against my bare lower back, he starts up my engines all over again.

"Showtime," I breathe.

It's a long night of watching him toss dough in the air and listening to customers clap and whoop and whistle. No wonder his arms are so sculpted. The man is the Harlem Globetrotters of pizza dough. At least once during each cycle of diners, he tosses a crust in the air and spins underneath it. I feel like he's going to try to roll it up in a ball and slam dunk it.

I thought it was vaguely cool before I knew the man. Now his skills make him sexy as hell.

And I'm losing my freaking mind. The upside here is I direct all my frustrations at learning how to knead dough. I knock the fuck out of it while Leo does what he does.

I'm covered in flour and sweat during a lull post-early-birds, and the pre-date-night crowd as the brick oven continues to radiate so much heat.

I'm also starving from the aroma of pizza but trying to ignore it as I clean up my workstation and prepare to make yet more dough for Leo.

Hands grab me from behind, and I yelp in surprise. Leo's arms are around my waist, and my feet are no longer on the floor. My feet don't touch terra firma again until I hear the door to his office slam shut behind us.

"Leo, what—"

This kiss, with me flat against the office door with no escape, is what I knew Leo had inside him from the second I laid eyes on him yesterday. His tongue prods my lips open, and I welcome him inside my mouth. I need this as much as he does.

My fingers have ached to comb through his thick hair;

now my hands clutch those astonishingly soft waves because I know how quickly this moment could end. His kiss is even more intense than his soul-stirring gaze. His eyes communicate volumes, but his kiss shows me everything beyond words. No one has ever kissed me like this before; it's a lover's kiss, the kind people get when someone has returned from war or something. An I-can't-get-enough-of-you kind of kiss. I'm ready to believe he means it and that I deserve it.

He sees me; he knows so much about me that I have been afraid to share with the people I love. And he sees past all of that and cares for me anyway.

Both of his hands are on my midsection, over the apron, and I miss the feel of his fingertips against my skin. I reach back and tug at my apron knot and pull the neck strap off over my head.

Leo smiles and rests his hands on my waist, brushing his fingers against my lower back, this time daring to creep up a little higher. The rough pads of his thumbs against my skin make my body tremble. I imagine what those work-worn thumbs will feel like rubbing against my nipples, against the untouched places below my navel—everywhere that needs to be touched. I'm suddenly lightheaded at the thought of his hands having their way with me. He's so beefy and masculine, yet so considerate; would he be rough or gentle with me? Something tells me I would enjoy it both ways.

I wait impatiently for him to resume the kissing, but first, he looks into my eyes and runs his thumb along my bottom lip.

"Someone should write an opera about this face."

My ears heat up, and I know just by the sensation that they are red as a Roma tomato. I'm not embarrassed; I hope he doesn't think that.

"I'm not used to people talking to me like this. It's going to take some time, Leo."

He leans in so close that when he speaks, I can feel his breath across my lips. "How about kissing? Are you used to being kissed like this?"

When he lays his mouth across mine again, my whole world turns to a welcome, velvety fog. My eyes are closed, but the void behind them is full of rainbows and glitter in the darkness. I am lost in this kiss. The contact between us builds so much heat inside me that by the time he teases with the tip of his tongue, my mind has turned to goo.

He licks once then pulls away. I have to force myself not to whimper.

"No," I say. "No one has ever kissed me like that."

He growls and kisses me again, murmuring in between prodding, warm, wet kisses. "No one else will."

His tongue fully slides into my mouth again and wakes up all the dormant corners of my body and mind. I want to experience all the things this man can do with my body now that he's woken me up.

As if reading my thoughts, Leo pulls away from the kiss one more time, his eyes hooded, his lips glistening from our kiss, and slides one thick thigh between my legs.

I draw in a deep breath at the wave of anticipation this creates in me. "I have to tell you something before this goes any further. Leo. I'm a virgin."

Leo takes less than a beat to respond. He looks intently at me and furrows his brow as if I'd suggested we eat raw pizza dough for breakfast.

Oh shit. Here it comes.

Chapter Twelve

Leo

DIANA LOOKS AWAY, biting her lip.

She's so unsure of herself, and I hate the idea that anyone put thoughts into her head that being a virgin is somehow a disadvantage.

"I can't imagine why you think that's an issue for me."

She glances back at me then looks past my head; she can't seem to meet my eyes.

"Some guys have broken up with me because of it. Because I wouldn't, you know, put out."

I palm the sides of her face with both my hands firmly. "Listen, there's nothing wrong with you. You are perfect exactly the way you are. And you're my girl. Understand?" She hesitantly nods.

I grit my teeth. "What do I have to do to convince you that it's not a big deal?"

She smirks. "Kiss me again."

Her playfulness and her tender lips pull a deep groan out of me as I lock our mouths together, pressing my pelvis tighter against her. She pushes back, and I grunt in longing at the friction.

"What can I do for you, Leo?"

"Come closer."

My heart threatens to knock itself silly right through my chest in response to the way she looks back at me. "I'm already here, I can't get any clos—"

"Let's test that theory," I say, rudely interrupting and hiking her legs up around my hips, grinding her against the door.

My Diana moans into my mouth, and returns grind for grind. My filthy brain is desperate to know if she's wet for me. And how wet?

Don't even think about dicking her in your office between the dinner rushes. She doesn't deserve that for her first time. And then the filthy voice reminds me, *You said yourself it wasn't a big deal. So just go for it. She's ready.*

I never would have thought I'd be thankful for my one of my brothers interrupting me while losing myself in this woman's affection.

But I'll say it, thank god Frank burst through the door of the office right before I got carried away.

Of course, he could have knocked first and prevented Diana and me from nearly tumbling to the floor.

"Leo!"

A scuffling noise accompanies Frank's voice. Diana gasps and hops down off me. She tries to scurry away, but I've got her. Drawing an arm around her and pulling her close, I tell her not to worry; he's my brother.

She looks at me with wide eyes. "I'm not ready to meet your family," she hisses.

"I'm sorry," I tell her. "But I didn't know he was gonna

show up like this. Anyway, Frank's cool. You'll like him." Frank's five o'clock shadow and the wild look in his blood-shot eyes don't make him look especially cool. What's even less okay is Diana's reaction to the dude he's got by the back of the shirt. Frank shoves the scrawny little fucker into a chair and looks at Diana.

He points to the scrawny dude, who looks both put out and scared. "This him?"

Diana presses a hand to her chest. "What is *he* doing here?" Then she pivots to me, fire in her eyes. "What *is* he doing here? What did you do?"

I raise my hands to call for a time out. "Hold on a minute. Let's make introductions. Frank? This is Diana.

Diana? This is my brother Frank."

Frank nods. "Nice to meet you. I'm sorry for startling you two lovebirds."

"Frank, please," I say.

"Moving on. I'm sorry to bother you, Diana, but is this the guy?"

She looks like she's still trying to collect her thoughts. "Judging by her reaction, I'd say yes. That's the guy who framed her for driving while impaired."

At that moment, Toby walks in. My manager freezes, eyeing this scene that's playing out without explanation. He points to Frank and then to me. "Am I interrupting a family meeting or…?"

Frank blurts, "Go get the lady a glass of water, would ya?"

Diana nods. "Yeah, I think I need a second."

She looks pale and not at all happy to see that punk-ass bitch Gary. No surprise there. When she sips the water, she looks from me to Frank to Gary and back to me. When she eventually composes herself, she starts with Gary.

"Explain yourself." Diana crosses her arms and sits

down in my chair behind my desk, waiting for Gary to say what she needs to hear him say.

Gary, still looking put upon, splutters, "I was just locking my door on the way to work, and this jerkoff starts roughing me up. Shoved me in the back of his creepy car with no locks and drove me here."

Diana levels him with a devastating sneer. "No, idiot. Explain to me what you did that night that I got picked up for DUI."

"I told you not to drive! I warned you!"

"Tell the truth, Gary."

Frank slowly cracks his knuckles one by one as if preparing for a fistfight. "Yeah, Gar. Tell the lady the truth, or I got a fun game you and I can play together. It's called Hide the Tooth. I knock out a tooth, and you have five minutes to find it before we go again." "Bit much, Frankie," I say.

He looks at me. "Think so?"

I nod. Frank shrugs. "Ah well. It's been a while since I interrogated a bitch. I got excited. I'll try to behave, as long as you tell the truth, Gar."

Gary cackles and points his chin at Diana. "You got a couple of pimps fighting over you now, is that it? I should have figured you'd end up this way."

It's not Frank who strikes first. Or me, even though I charge at him before I can stop myself.

Diana hits first and hits hard.

The chair tumbles on its side in the scuffle, and Diana pins Gary to the wall, her fist full of his stupid tee-shirt.

Her other hand cracks him one time in the nose. I know that noise, and it's about to get ugly in here.

Blood pours out and the scrawny dude cries like a baby. "Okay, okay, I'll tell you! Just don't punch me again. And tell your pimps to back off."

Diana, with an eerie calm, turns to me. "Leo?"

"Yeah, baby?"

"Hit him again for me, would you? That hurt my hand."

She doesn't have to ask me twice.

Chapter Thirteen

Diana

IT FEELS good to have my name cleared, not just because my court fees have gone away.

Justice feels good.

After Gary spilled the truth—it only took one more knock to the head—Frank took him down to the precinct, and Leo and I followed while Leo's assistant chef took over the late dinner shift.

After a couple of hours' worth of paperwork and interviews, the police tell me I'm free to go. All charges are dropped.

Outside the precinct, Leo slips his arms around my waist and gives me that soulful gaze that I'm gradually becoming more comfortable with.

"We'd better get back to work, huh, boss? Don't want to disappoint the dinner crowd."

Leo shakes his head. "You have the rest of the night off

and so do I. My assistant chef can do it just as well as I can, and I think we earned it."

My lips must be sending the signal they want Leo to kiss them again, because he does just that. The tenderness is a beautiful feeling after spending all evening in an institutional gray space under the scrutiny of the police, in between long periods of waiting and doing nothing. Of course, being in a waiting room with Leo is not exactly dull.

He kept my hand in his the whole time, except to fetch me water and coffee. He took my mind off the waiting with stories about his childhood, and had me tell him all about mine and my crazy family of five sisters.

When the police insisted he had to stay in the waiting room while I gave my testimony to the investigators in the interview room, Leo was adorably grumpy about having to leave my side even for a minute. Oddly, the waiting area of the precinct was the best first date of my life, I tell him.

Five stars. Would recommend.

"Oh, you mean, best second date. Our first date was when you ralphed in my Jeep," he teases.

I punch his bulbous shoulder, and he pretends it hurts. "Forget driving; you gotta get a license for that right hook, young lady."

I roll my eyes, but I can't stop smiling all the way back to his house.

We're having such a good time that I pout like a preteen when he shows me to my room, yet he doesn't come in.

I smooth my hand up Leo's chest. "But I'm ready now," I say.

He pulls me close and kisses me for what must be the hundredth time that day. "I know. But I made plans while you were talking to the cops. Now go rest up and get dressed. I'll come and fetch you when it's time for our third date."

He leaves, and looking around this large guest room, I feel a strange familiarity. That's when I notice my favorite fuzzy blanket is on the bed. "What the?"

I go to the closet, and all my clothes are on hangers, as well as a pretty summer dress displayed prominently that I've never seen before.

In the adjoining bathroom, it's more of my stuff, in addition to a basket full of new lotions and potions that I've only seen in magazines and could never afford.

"All my shit is here," I say to Chloe when I call her. "I think he moved me out of the motel and into his house." I expect her to be horrified at Leo's forwardness. "Thank god. That place has been the site of at least three murders we know about."

"You overreact about the wrong things. I was sort of wondering if you were going to try to talk me out of moving so quickly with Leo."

Chloe pauses for a moment, then says, "Let's see. I met my husband, and three days later, we were engaged. So, no, I don't see myself telling you to run away. You sound happy; that's all I care about."

"I am. Cautiously."

"Don't be too cautious. You are a virgin at 25."

I laugh. "Oh, I'm definitely going to jump Leo's bones tonight."

Chapter Fourteen

Leo

THE SPECIAL PIZZA that we made together today—
the one
Diana had spilled an entire jar of tomato sauce over—I
had delivered to the house for our date.

On the veranda overlooking the pool, we demolish half
of the pizza while we comfortably wind our way through a
dozen or more important topics of conversation: favorite
movies, books, music, how many kids each of us wants,
and the proper way to eat an Oreo cookie.

"I thought that dress I had delivered was pretty, but
you make it look amazing," I tell her.

Diana looks away shyly again, and a flush of pink
blooms across her chest, muting the rainbow skull tattoo.

"Look at me."

"I'm not used to all this attention, Leo."

I slip my hands around both of hers and draw them to
my lips, pressing a kiss to each of her knuckles. "Get used

to it quickly because I can't stop looking at you, touching you, thinking about you."

"You're kind of a lot, Leo. But I like it."

I continue my kisses across the back of her hand, down to her wrist, up her forearm. I want to kiss every inch of her; every bit of my Diana sets my soul on fire. "I knew as soon as I saw you that you were mine, Diana. All day long, it killed me to look and not touch."

She laughs. "You did your share of touching."

"I could not wait to get you alone," I say, unable to deny it, dotting her collarbones with slow, wet kisses.

"You're a bad influence," she teases. "I've been having nothing but dirty thoughts since you dropped me off last night."

Kissing up her neck and back down to the little valley between her breasts, I have to know what that means.

"What kind of dirty thoughts?"

Diana moans when I nose the fabric aside to nuzzle one breast.

She answers, "I've been thinking about riding those thighs since last night."

"Do it," I reply instantly, now focusing on the other breast. One slight tug, and I notice something amid my nuzzling. Diana's not wearing a bra under her dress. I growl and tease her with my lips through the thin, soft fabric, nudging and nuzzling until her nipple rises up to say hello. "There you are," I say, running my thumb over it, teasing it out more, tasting and savoring her soft skin.

"Oh," she says, like she's surprised I'm into the idea.

"Really? Here, on the veranda?"

"Get on this thing," I say, slapping my thigh. Something's come over me, and I'm soon blurting out all sorts of filth I never imagined would come out of my mouth. "I want you to smear that wet virgin pussy all over my legs."

"Wow. Just, wow," she says, her breath going shaky.

Diana doesn't hesitate another second; she pushes back her patio chair, climbs up, and straddles my leg, squeezing it between her thighs.

I can't help but notice two things: one, how nice it is to have this woman's boobs in my face. The second thing has my mouth salivating and my cock twitching angrily.

"Baby," I rumble, still nuzzling and petting her breasts, "You're not wearing a single thing under that dress. Not even panties."

"You're right, boss. Do I get my bonus now?"

I like this. I mean, I really like this thing Diana's doing.

"Be a good girl and ride me, just like that, until you come. I want to watch your face the whole time." She wets her lips and steals my heart with her kiss. "Yes, sir," she says, then leans back and lets me watch.

I keep my eyes on her face, watching every changing expression while she rides my thigh. She closes her eyes and parts her lips, reveling in the friction.

"That's it, girl. Get it. Fucking come on my leg." My teeth grit, my skin tightens, and my angry-red cock jerks inside my chinos.

Diana is so beautiful and becomes even more so when she orgasms. She falls against me, digging her nails into my back through my shirt.

"That's my girl."

"Leo," she gasps, her body still quaking. "I've ruined your pants."

"I need them off now. And that dress needs to get gone. And before you ask, the answer is yes. Here. On the veranda. Now."

Chapter Fifteen

Diana

LEO TAKES his time with me, blocking the world out with his big arms around my naked body. I don't remember if I've ever been naked outdoors before, but the breeze and his eyes roaming my curves make me feel safe and cherished.

He catches me looking down between our bodies.

"Touch it, Diana. It's just a penis."

He makes me laugh, but my tittering stops when I hold his throbbing red dick in my hand. Its velvety softness on the outside surprises me, despite it standing erect.

Extremely, demandingly erect.

Leo makes me blush with his frankness. He walks me through the process, just like he did with kneading the dough earlier today. "Come up a little," he whispers.

I rise up a bit on my knees, and he slides his hand inside my folds. My body twitches at this new sensation, his rough fingers igniting fresh need in my most sensitive flesh.

He grunts out a small curse. "My good girl is so wet; she might win employee of the month."

I once again have the urge to grind; the ache builds so quickly while he touches and explores my pussy.

"Already on my first day?" I ask breathily, giving him as much playful innocence as I can muster even though my insides are screaming for him to rail me.

"Well," he says, sliding one digit into my channel.

"Maybe I should break you in slowly first."

I squeak at the feeling of his finger filling me, and then a second. The in-and-out motion delivers heat to every corner of my body. Every nerve ending feels awake with arousal. "Do you…oh god…think I'm a good fit?"

He laughs, withdrawing his fingers. I cry out in frustration because I need more. It's a deep, primal need so intense it almost hurts. Instead, he centers me above the tip of his cock, and then holds my gaze while he uses his hand to drench his entire throbbing length in my juices.

"You tell me, young lady. Do you think you can follow orders?"

"Yes, chef."

"Good girl. Now, take it. But go easy."

I try, I really do. I get an A for effort. But I just can't get the correct angle. Tears well up in my eyes.

"Hey. It's okay. We can stop, Diana."

I shake my head and smile. "I think I need you to show me how to slide it just right in the oven the first time, chef."

He chuckles and kisses me softly. "I love you," he blurts.

I gasp. "What?" Did he really just say that?

"It's official. Your boss is a human resources nightmare. I hope you won't file a complaint," he says.

Oh. So, we're still playing the game. Phew. I think.

"Depends on how fast he can flip me over and shut me up with that big red pepperoni sausage."

Both of us laugh while Leo's also half-snarling, and I'm flat on my back on the patio sofa. Leo's strong hands spread me wide, kneading my sore thighs. I'm not expecting his head to dip down for a taste, and my body jerks once again at the unexpected touch. So attentive Leo is, getting me accustomed to this with sweet, gentle kisses and licks, though there's nothing delicate about my body's reaction. One tender kiss against my clit, and my second orgasm slams into me. I cry out, though I don't hear any sounds. Everything around me feels like it's buzzing with joy. My body is on fire with newfound energy.

And then I'm free. I just came, twice, outside, on my boss's veranda. As wrong as the world says it is to boink my boss, it's more than right for me. Not just the sex, but the way he makes me feel is all kinds of right and proper. The way he sees me and accepts me for me. I only hope I can make him feel half as good.

Soon, I relax into this moment and enjoy Leo's mouth on my pussy, his tongue diving into my cunt, his whole face ravishing every inch of me.

I happen to look down. I shouldn't have done that. His heated, slicked face, the wild look in his eyes. He's watching me. Still. As always. It's too much, too intense, and I come again. How? How is he doing this to me?

With one wicked kiss, he towers above me. "One thing you always do in the kitchen. Taste as you go." When he kisses my mouth and shares my sticky sweetness with me, I know what he means by that. Oh. My. God. I don't know if he should be congratulated or arrested for that comment.

I don't get the chance to punch him for that; he's got one of my legs thrown over one of his big shoulders, and the tip of his cock teases my entrance. Once again, he lubes his length with my juice and begins to ease in.

Inch by inch, he tortures me. Going deeper, then pulling out, pausing to watch my reaction, kissing me, then sinking in a little bit more.

"Relax your muscles. You've been a good girl. Working very hard."

Just the word "relax" from him opens me up, and he pushes past my barrier. It doesn't even hurt as much as I expect it to.

Gently he begins a slow rhythm, gliding in and out of me, his gaze locked on my face, studying every flinch, every expression.

"What does my good employee think? Is she a team player? Gonna stick around for the long haul?"

I smile wickedly and grind into him, demanding a faster pace. "On one condition. I want overtime without prior approval."

He gives me one deliciously rough thrust. "Done."

"And I want all the sausage. I'm the only one who's allowed to touch it."

Another, harder thrust, with one rough hand gripping my soft hip so tight, and the other holding us steady on the rickety patio sofa. The cushions start to give way; soon he'll be fucking me on bare metal, and I do not care. "As if that were ever a question," he says. "You're the only sausage handler I want."

I dig my nails into his back as my legs squeeze. I want him deeper, rougher. My Leo knows. He pulls out and drives back in, sending cushions flying and the sofa legs scraping against the tile.

"I'm gonna come, baby."

"Not yet. First, you have to tell me if I can come in late tomorrow. You worked me to the bone tonight, chef."

Leo's wild and red-faced now, his eyes watery. Another pump and his warm release floods me, just as he's released a flood of love into my life.

"My good girl gets everything she asks for," he says, voice barely a rattle against my chest. I curl around him, keeping him inside, not ready to let him go.

I'll never be ready to let him go.

"I wasn't messing around before, Diana. I love you."

Looking into his eyes, I see now we're done with our little game.

"Leo, I'm going to love you forever."

Another kiss, this time sweet and soul-affirming.

"Thank you."

I can hardly believe this man is thanking me, after everything he's done.

"Thank you for letting me take care of you."

A lump erupts in my throat. "Oh. That. You're welcome?" I can't help it; I have to laugh. It feels absurd to thank someone for making space to help. But I get it, in a way. I get it because I get Leo, and he gets me.

Curled up in his lap moments later, Leo has us wrapped in a blanket and the cushions back where they belong. "A crisscross imprint on my balls didn't seem fun," he jokes.

I snort. "Well, you didn't have to scare the cushions away."

"I'm a scary dude."

"You're a teddy bear. Your brother, on the other hand…."

"Oh, by the way. You're coming with me to the family reunion."

"You say that like I don't have a choice," I tease.

He shrugs. "Frank already met you, which means my

other two brothers and sister, my parents, and my grandparents are probably blowing my phone up by now."

"I haven't heard any calls."

He smooths my hair out of my face. "My phone gets turned off when I'm fucking my wife."

"What?!"

He blanches. "I mean my girlfriend."

I look into his eyes, and I know that's not what he meant.

For the first time, I'm not scared.

"You can call me whatever you like. I'm down for anything, Leo. As long as anything is with you. Just don't ever torture me again like you did today at work."

Leo stands and lifts me, blanket and all, into his arms. Moments later, he's kicking open his bedroom door and tossing my stretched, exhausted body onto a bed covered in soft pillows and blankets. Like I said, solid arms and legs.

"So, tell me, Diana. Where do you see yourself in five years?"

"Somewhere about here," I reply, tugging on his chest hair.

"Achievable goal," he says with a wince and a laugh. "I fully support it."

All Abby's books are stand-alone romances, each with its own HEA. No cliffhangers or cheating!

Abby's latest releases:

Fix Me Up

(single dad, family doctor)

Followed by the CEO

(insta obsession, 'fun' stalking)

Filthy Chef

(workplace romance/one-night-stand-turned HEA)

Reckless Royals

Favored Prince (royal family/American bride)

Bad Prince (forced marriage/divorce pact)

Wild Prince (Forced proximity)

Forgotten Prince (mariage pact)

Stolen Crown (brother's best friend)

Related short story: Reckless in Ruins

Roadside Attractions series:

Roadside Attraction (insta love)

Claiming Fate (rivals to lovers)

Falling into Fate (long lost friends to lovers)

Fate's Dark Shadows (age gap)

Rode Hard (insta love, dating app)

Crash into Me (grumpy mountain man)

Snowed Under (second chance, later-in-life)

Wish List (holiday, older heroine/younger hero)

Fate's Holi-Date (he falls first, age gap)

Wood Brothers series

(OTT alpha insta-love. Set in same world as Roadside Attractions.)

Nailed

Screwed

Drilled

Love Games series

(OTT insta love, nerdy-but-hot heroes. Set in same world as Roadside Attractions.)

Roll For Initiative

Roll for Damage

Roll for Charisma

The Mail-Order Brides of Darling Creek

(tropes include: age gap, mail/e-mail order brides, small town, insta love, cowboy)

A Baby for the Bride

A Week to Wed

Her Guardian Groom

The Cowboy Auction of Darling Creek

(tropes include: dating auction, small town, cowboy, insta love)

The Cowgirl's Bid

Winning the Cowboy

Her Forbidden Prize

Small-Town Gossip

(Set in Darling Creek, Montana. Tropes include: small town, insta love, workplace romance)

Do That To Me

Say That To Me

Love That For Me

Paradise Passions

(vacation romances)

Babymoon

Honeymoon Hideout

Need more stand alones?

Are You For Reel?

The Bodyguard and His Bunny

A Little Amusement

511 Kissme Lane

V-Card Vacation

Hail Mary

Holiday short reads

Elf-napped

Bagged by the Elf

Wish List

Snow-plowed

The Christmas Pickup

The Halloween Bet

The Halloween Flip

Pumpkin King

Snow-plowed

Additional titles are available on iBooks, Barnes & Noble, Everand, Smashwords, Fable, and more.

For signed paperbacks, exclusive downloads, and more, visit Abby's website at authorabbyknox.com

Happy reading!

Epilogue

Leo

FIVE YEARS later

I DIDN'T BOTHER to tell Diana five years ago when we got together that my family reunion is in Sicily, on my family's ancestral vineyard.

She didn't seem bothered when the revelation came while we waited in international departures a few weeks later.

When our two oldest girls are four and three years old, old enough to start making memories, Diana and I host the family Christmas at the vineyard. The Williamses, all their spouses and kids, have their own small villa on the property. My side of the family has decided to join us, and they're all bunking in the main inn on the grounds.

There's no snow, but I'm hoping the free-flowing wine,

unlimited homemade local cuisine, and acres of land for the kids to explore will make up for it.

As the two families gather around the enormous table in the courtyard on a mercifully balmy December night, Diana's dad gives a toast.

As always, I keep an eye on my wife, who's feeding our infant son at her breast. I adjust the blanket around her to keep them warm and refill her water glass.

"It's not a traditional Christmas for the Williamses, but I think I speak for all the Williamses when I say we're honored to be a part of a family to introduce us to new traditions."

After a boisterous "Saluti," we dig into the traditional four-course meal. Later, my mom and grandmother deliver the desserts to the table. My grandmother, never one to mince words, looks skeptically at what Chloe's husband, Phillip, has added to the celebration. "I've never had a suet brick for Christmas," Grandma says with a shrug.

"Diana, who's never quite lost her snark, says, "Oh wow, Phillip. Is that the same cake you brought to

Christmas last year?"

"Not the actual same one. I make a new one every year," Phillip insists.

Cecily's husband stifles a laugh, and Cecily shushes him.

Chloe pats Phillip on the shoulder. "Poor dear. He keeps trying every year, and every year no one eats the

Christmas cake."

Cherise mutters, "Why would we when we're already drunk on good wine, and that thing will give us all alcohol poisoning."

Every year, poor Phillip tries, and every year, not even his own wife will touch the stuff.

I feel bad for the guy. "All right. I'll try it."

About ten people shout "No!" at me as I take a bite.

"I don't know what everyone's problem is. It's not that bad."

The truth is, it's also not great. Spicy, pungent, damp, nutty, fruity? Yes. Tasty? Meh.

"Thank you, Leo," says Phillip, raising his wine glass.

"It's a tough crowd," I say, returning the gesture.

Chloe shrugs. "Oh no, Leo took a bite. You'll have to make a whole new one next year, honey."

Phillip sets his glass down on the table with a firm clink and turns to his wife. "I told you, it's not the same exact one."

"Potato, potahto."

I watch, curious, as Phillip leans in and whispers something in Chloe's ear. She blushes deep red, then pushes back her chair. "Excuse me, everyone."

The four sisters groan; everyone else looks confused but carries on with dessert.

I turn to Diana. "What's going on?" I mutter. She laughs and beckons me to come closer.

"It's a game. Chloe refuses Christmas cake, and he takes her away for a spanking."

Shocked, I blurt. "Wow. Wow. Huh. You don't say. That's very interesting."

"Husband, why are you babbling? Are you drunk?"

I answer, "Enough to give me an idea."

A smile creeps across my wife's face. "What idea?"

I lean in and murmur for her ears only. "I think we're overdue for an employee of the month ceremony."

Diana's eyes widen with a familiar flash. Quickly, she unlatches the milk-drunk little Leo Jr. from her breast, covers up, and wordlessly hands our sleeping babe over to my mother.

She grabs my hand and marches me to our suite.

Five minutes later, I'm eight inches deep into my best employee, who's requesting more overtime.

"Please, chef? I still have art school debt to pay."

"I'm too thirsty to decide. Be a good girl and get me something to drink."

My wife's muscles tighten around me when we do that special secret thing we like. The thing she got shamed for when she brought it up in a mommy group discussion about post-pregnancy sex. We decided shortly thereafter that mommy group was too uptight for Diana.

My suckling at each of her heavy breasts draws a moan from her lips, while my thumb reaches between us and strums her to completion.

"Leo!"

My wife bucks against me and digs her nails in my back, and I still love the exquisite pain of it. She lets me have my fill of her, while I fill her up with my seed.

I joyfully clean her up with my tongue while my eyes stay locked on hers.

"Employee of the month? Employee of the fucking century."

I toss my girl on her back with one swift move, ready to give her a second reward.

"Pizza man better be careful tossing me around.

Another ten years? I might break a hip."

I pause, resting my head against the pillowy curve of her breasts, breathing in her scent, wondering what that skull tattoo will look like in another ten, twenty, or thirty years. I can't wait to find out.

"You know I'll always be here to catch you, Diana."

THE END

Thank you for reading Hand Tossed! If you enjoyed this story, please visit my website at authorabbyknox.com for information about more titles to read. Want to know more about Diana's pastry chef sister Cherise and her sexy boss, Bishop? Read Chef's Kiss next. Homemade Heat reading order:

Judge Me
Cake Walk
Hand-Tossed
Chef's Kiss
Bite Me

About the Author

Abby Knox writes feel-good, high-heat romance that readers have described as quirky, sexy, adorable, and hilarious.

Abby's favorite tropes include: Forced proximity, opposites attract, grumpy/sunshine, age gap, boss/employee, fated mates/insta-love, and more. Abby is heavily influenced by Buffy the Vampire Slayer, Gilmore Girls, and LOST. But don't worry, she won't ever make you suffer like Luke & Lorelai.

Say hello at authorabbyknox@gmail.com

www.ingramcontent.com/pod-product-compliance
Lightning Source LLC
Chambersburg PA
CBHW072032150726
47999CB00002B/857